The Cyborg Merman

By Amanda Milo

Copyright © 2020 Amanda Milo ALL RIGHTS RESERVED. This book contains material protected under International and Federal Copyright Laws and Treaties. Any unauthorized reprint or use of this material is prohibited. No part of this book may be reproduced, distributed, or transmitted in any form or by any means, electronic or mechanical, including photocopying, recording, or by an information and retrieval system without express written permission from the Author/Publisher except in the case of brief quotations embodied in critical reviews and certain other noncommercial uses permitted by copyright law. This is a work of fiction. Names, characters, places, and incidents either are the product of the author's imagination or are used fictitiously, and any resemblance to actual persons, living or dead, business establishments, events, or locales is entirely coincidental.
Edited by LY Services

Special Thanks To...

L ori Morris, for your kind words. And to Beasab, for the same.

To my better half, who lets me complicate his life and says he's lucky for it.

WARNING:

You might have seen the words 'Dub-con' in the blurb—
(If you bought this without even reading the blurb **GOD LOVE YOU!** *Heart Eyes*)

—Dub-con is short for Dubious Consent, a category of romance books that typically includes a scene or is based on the premise of one party not consenting to sexual activity.

If this kind of material would trigger you, I UNDERSTAND—and it's with the kindest suggestion that I tell you to close this book now. Pass on this story. You don't need that stress. I've got some fully, 110% Otterly Safe consenting books coming up soon! <3

Love,
Amanda♥

CHAPTER 1

STELLA

My husband has been dead for a month. On the frontier planet of Traxia, that's a small lifetime for a woman to be single, and it isn't unheard of for a widow of one week to remarry. It's the way of life here: on this planet's surface, we've harkened back to something like the days of Earth's Westward Expansion. In a lot of ways, it's *exactly* like those long ago days on that faraway planet.

Traxia is in the process of being terraformed. Men were dropped here to establish it, to carve out an existence in this harsh new corner of the galaxy. A lot of modern tech doesn't work here. Communication gets no fancier than paper letters in most areas, although some devices get enough reception in bigger cities.

We—

...I mean, *me*. Just me now. I'm in a ranching district. Our ranch *is* this district. The closest civilization is a mining town, and it's our ranch who puts the meat on the locals' tables.

And miners are hungry men. A metal similar in properties to gold was found a year or so back, and it's been a hive of activity, a modern-day 'gold' rush for the area, ever since. Baron and I—

Just me.

I raise a hybrid version of cattle, the meat of which is in even higher demand if I can drive our stock up to the markets even further outside of the region.

The cattle are similar enough in looks to Earthen cattle. The rest is Nfurian, a tough monsterish bovine native to the planet. To survive the constantly harsh climate, the cows are tough and mean, and their bulls are even meaner. Their meat though is sublime. We run eight thousand head and were lucky enough to end up on land with a river and a natural spring with water so pure you can drink it from your cupped hands, no treatment needed. It's priceless.

It may be worth killing over.

I'd be naïve if I didn't look at Baron's business partner and wonder if he killed my husband in order to secure the rights to our water. In a region as arid as ours, water is more precious than the metal veins the miners are making fortunes off of. Our water means we're rich as panners, because sure it's only a commodity and not a precious metal—but men still get stupid over it.

Although Kashykc'vest Ithor, or C'vest as my husband referred to his partner since we settled here, is not a stupid man.

...If you can call him a man, that is. He's technically a cyborg.

He's a cybernetic system created from an otherworldly-planet creature. An ocean humanoid called a Yonderin—

Essentially, an alien merman in the flesh.

—who started life with a tail rather than lower limbs, but now he has two artificial legs called *C-legs,* a term that is aurally ironic since he's originally from the sea himself.

His eyes, ears, and gill slits have had changes wrought upon them too, referred to as 'upgrades.' He can see, hear, and breathe on land just like the rest of us. But... a lot of locals are freaked out by what's essentially a fish-man walking around like a person. Frankly, most humans have an aversion to cyborgs, period.

Chilly reception aside, I can understand why his people altered their designs to leave the ocean. They're an incredibly advanced society, but limited in their scope of control. On their planet, the only way to direct what happened on land was to alter their people to survive on surfaces where they could act for the greater interest. Now their cyborgs have spread out, like C'vest. How C'vest ended up on a terraforming planet with a naturally arid climate is a mystery—I mean, why the hell would you stay?

But I've never asked him why. Technically, I've said very few words to the man, although Baron has worked closely with him for years. I've made breakfast with C'vest in mind, serving the few seaside dishes we can occasionally get ahold of the ingredients to make from time to time. That way, he'd feel a little slice of home as he talked business with my mate at the dining table.

Now I'm sitting across from him wondering if he murdered my husband.

C'vest looks mostly human in his face, although his skin appears to have rougher textures and next to no weathering, no gathering of sun wrinkles. His features are handsome, I suppose, in that way that powerful creatures are. His eyes are usually dark, like shark's eyes. Occasionally they light up with blue flares. Flares that snake out in circuit-symmetry patterns as he receives biofeedback. As you can imagine, the sight of his dark eyes beginning to glow doesn't make him look less imposing. Neither does his height, which is enough alone to make him cut a formidable figure. When he walks, his long prosthetic legs eat up the ground, his gait measured. In no way is it a swagger; it's probably the effect of his biosystem efficiently traversing whatever plane he's striding across, using all precision. But the effect is a man who has pure confidence. And today, dressed in a collared dress shirt, a red vest, pinstriped pants, and his black-dyed leather duster, he's intimidating.

He did take his hat off at the door (along with the duster). But that's less about making himself look less threatening and more due to decent manners. He has excellent manners.

We're sitting in the wingback chairs my husband and I have had since we were gifted them by his parents when we got married. When C'vest entered the room, suspecting what I suspect he's done, I was prepared to crack a whiskey bottle over his head if he dared to sit in the chair that Baron always claimed.

He didn't though. C'vest took the same chair he always has. The one he used when he was here for business or to shoot the breeze with Baron.

It feels like he's prepared to speak about business matters now. I uncurl my fingers from my fists and smooth them down my jean-clad legs. For years, I've worn dresses because Baron appreciated the look of me in feminine things. He was a throwback to another time in a very far off place, and it didn't bother me to indulge him. He made me feel pretty. And in a place this rough, it was a special kind of comfort at the end of the day for Baron to come home to me and envelop himself in my softness.

I've been in jeans since the day he died.

Chiefly because it isn't safe for me to look any softer or gentler than I already do, being a woman. A lone woman. Just as if we've been transported back in time, it's old world laws that hold sway around here. Which is frustrating. And for me, dangerous. Because when a man dies, everything goes to his widow. If she remarries, everything gets turned over to her new husband. There's another twist to that law, but the gist is: it means the sharks are circling.

I look C'vest right in his weirdly lit blue-circuit eyes.

They haven't faded to black once since he's sat down. It's unnerving me. "Why are you here, C'vest?"

His mouth tightens imperceptibly at the corners. "I haven't heard that name since Baron died. He was the only one to use it. And you."

I stare at him.

He nods once, his hands cupped over his square-shaped knees, mechanics covered by cyberskin draped in cotton fabric. "I've come here with your best interests in mind."

I keep staring at him.

His eyes are glowing brighter than ever as he studies me, so uncharacteristically silent. I've never had reason to sit down and shoot the breeze with C'vest but I was a good hostess. Pleasant. Warm.

Now?

C'vest leans forward, elbows planting on his thighs. The leaned-forward posture lowers his height some, but he's still taller than me by a head and a half. "We need to get married."

My throat seizes. Even though I had a precognitive sense and a wild idea of where this conversation would go, I feel the betrayal like he's clamped his fist around my throat.

His eyes fade to Stygian black before flashing to active lines of glowing blue data. "I know that for you, it isn't ideal—"

My attempt to swallow just lodges a harder knot in the back of my throat.

"—however, with the local laws being what they are, you're in danger. Baron wouldn't want to see you get hurt."

Anger *lunges* inside me, like a mad dog busting free of its chain. I'm furious that he's invoking Baron's name to manipulate me.

"*I* don't want to see you hurt." His gaze meets mine, so solemn that I can almost believe him.

"The locals all know that Baron is gone. They're more than aware that all they need to do is marry you to acquire your water rights, along with every oxyoke of land—"

An oxyoke is a standard measurement of land here. It's the area you can plow with a yoke of oxen in one day's worth of work.

"—and every head of cattle you now solely own." His face, in its compelling perfection, is arranged in grave lines. "And so I must ask: Stella, will you marry me?"

What he's said is true. I *am* in danger. I've hardly done anything outside of the house for the operation—not fence repairs, not medicating steers, nothing that requires two hands—because I've had to keep one hand on the gun strapped to my hip. Baron's gun. Our ranch hands, a mix of humans and aliens, men who were loyal to my husband before he died, still work the ranch. But if it was dangerous to be alone with any of them before, it would be asinine now.

Proving he knows exactly what the recent danger has been, C'vest's already down-turned mouth tightens even more. "As you're aware, if any of the men here want to gain the holdings that now belong to you, they can circumvent your consent to marriage. I would spare you that," he says softly. His gaze is steady on mine.

He means they could rape me.

Here on Traxia, our laws are *real* old school. If a woman is raped, the man can be punished with death. But if the man is willing to pay a fine to her family, he can marry her and avoid the death penalty.

Among women, it's often referred to as the 'marry-your-rapist' law, and although it's something I only ever heard about on Earth, it's a rule alive and doing horrifically well here.

It's supposed to slow a man down from taking a woman against her will. Make him accountable. Give him consequences he has to think about before he rashly tosses her down and rips her skirt up. Because here, the man also has to lawfully care for said wife for the rest of her days if he takes her as his. Unless she dies, she's his full responsibility, and here's the kicker: he only ever gets *one*.

If he kills her, he doesn't get the approval to remarry. And if he rapes another woman, he hangs for it.

In this case, where there's much to gain, the threat of the noose if the court denies the guy would be worth risking to some men. A man might think the odds of him being granted access to land with water, a fortune of cattle, and a woman to warm his bed and wet his cock for the rest of his life is a pretty sweet deal. A deal so sweet, they'd hurt me for it, no hesitation.

I've already unholstered the gun twice when I've been amongst the ranch hands. It was enough to make them rethink edging any closer, but I'm afraid it won't last. I know I can't go on like this forever. For the most part, I've kept myself locked inside the house, and I never go out after dark anymore. Not for anything. Since the day Baron died, I've been living in heartsick sadness and pit-black fear.

Legally, I can live my life a successful cattle baroness and never remarry.

Practically, I won't last a year before some man with hunger for money, land, and power takes everything from me. And he'll humble me to do it.

That's how it's referred to when people are trying to be polite. *'He 'humbled' her.'*

What bullshit. Faced with the unholy greed and the cruelty slithering across men's faces—men who shook my husband's hand, who were loyal to him, who always tipped their hats to me, the bossman's wife—I can't help but think that *humble* is a word too far removed to convey the degradation, the *suffering* that's coming.

They were good men once. Probably still have lots of good left in them. But with a million credits' worth of land and two million in cattle on the table... It's enough to darken even decent hearts.

"I vow to you that I wouldn't be here now to ask this." When my gaze narrows, those blue chasing lines in C'vest's eyes brighten, his circuitry reading me, his eyes, which were designed to scope the ocean deep, now enhanced enough to scrutinize my every microexpression. "I wouldn't be here so soon," he amends. "I hoped to give you more time, but..." His chin drops, his jaw working, then jutting out as he takes in a deep breath. "But I overheard men in town talking. Alvert Galensten plans to have your agreement, and I quote, *'one way or another.'*"

I can't stop the shudder that travels up my spine.

"Exactly," C'vest says, not missing my reaction. "I wouldn't leave him alone with my horse, let alone you. Add to that, he hated Baron, and he hates me just as much. Probably more. I don't think he cares for Yonderin or approves of cyborgs. I wouldn't leave you to him if I could help it, and even if I thought he'd be good to you, I can kiss any hope of a future partnership goodbye if it's the likes of him taking the reins of your operation."

Numbness creeps over me. It's a familiar blanket lately. At first, I cried. I cried so much I thought the old saying about dying of a broken heart might be true. Might be possible. But a merciful death didn't happen for me. And I can't process the world I have to live in. I can't handle that these are my options. Be raped and get married, or get married and probably be raped. Wholly belong to some man. To a man who isn't Baron.

Ten years was all we got, Baron. How? We were *good* together. We were so happy. We should have shared a lifetime.

"Stella? Will you agree to marry me?"

C'vest has posed it so politely as a yes or no question. Instead of those two options, what escapes my mouth instead is a choked whisper. "Did you kill him?"

My focus returns sharply, honing in on C'vest's face for any flicker as I wait for him to answer.

His brows pinch briefly. That's it. That's his only reaction, save for his chin firming just slightly. "No, Stella. I didn't. Baron was my friend."

I'm not sure what I was hoping for. I guess I wanted his reaction to be overwhelmingly believable. Preferably in the negative, I wish I could say, but I think what I really wanted was for him to admit fault so that I had someone to attack. Someone to blame. Someone to hurt like I'm hurting. It was labeled a heart attack, and it could have been. But it isn't only me who wonders if it was no accident. Baron was a powerful man. A very rich man. There are few who stood to gain as much as C'vest did with his death.

From the business side of things, everything that can be rolled to C'vest already has been. Everything he was owed from their joint partnership has been squared.

Now it's a matter of the rest of it. Like crows circling a dead body, they will caw and pick away until the carcass is clean.

"Stella?" C'vest's hand lightly covers mine on my thighs and I jerk away like he's burned me. "Your hands are like ice," he declares, his voice rising slightly, almost sounding concerned. *"Stella,"* he says, his tone becoming imploring when I don't respond. "Listen to me. This is the most logical option."

Logical. I want to snarl at him, but C'vest has always been this way. Either it's his cyborg side or it's the alienness of him, but Baron has always said C'vest approaches the whole world differently. He's analytical to the point of seeming cold sometimes.

Calmly, unaware of the depth of my turmoil, he continues, "If I could afford to buy you out, I would. But my money is tied up in my own ventures."

"I could sell to someone else," I offer faintly. Because I know it's unlikely. Not many around here have the kind of capital to buy me out. And if they do, why would they? Why pay me when they could take me and then get *everything* for free?

"This is horrible," I choke out.

C'vest looks like he genuinely agrees with me. "You are correct. And it isn't right. But we can make the best of your options."

Hollowly, I share, "I loved him."

"I... know." And C'vest does look sorry. He looks as sorry as an aquatic species of alien-turned-man can.

"I don't love you," I protest.

"I know that too."

"I can't do this!" I cry, boiling to my feet.

C'vest surges up too. To my shock, he takes me by my upper arms. His face is more animated than I've ever seen it. He's scowling but not angry. He's determined and everything in his face and posture is urgency. "Stella, you *have* to. You need to make a definitive decision, and you're out of time to decide what that decision will be. Do you want to return to your home planet?"

"To my parents?" I've never been this close to C'vest before. For some reason, I always expected to catch the scent of fish on him, but it's fresh ocean waves that hit me instead. He smells almost as good as sunning in the ocean breeze, feeling cool damp sand squeeze between my toes as I bury my feet to keep them from burning.

"If you like."

I blink, thinking of my parents, who are back on Earth. Overcrowded, rioting Earth. Things have gone to hell there, making this place look like—if not paradise, then at least freer. I don't want to go back—I tried to get my parents *here*. Where there's space and quiet and opportunities to change yourself. No matter what my parents think, it's not so bad here... as long as you aren't a woman, that is. Maybe I should go home. But it's going to cost a small fortune for the transport fare. Unfortunately, Baron never kept that sort of credit cache sitting around. Most of our money is on four hooves and moos. And sadly, I can't just drive a herd of cattle up to the gate of the shuttleport and trade them for a ticket home. "I could try to sell what I have here, liquidate what I can."

"Yes."

And I would face the same problem: who here is going to *pay* me for anything when they can just *take* it?

"Damn it," I whimper raggedly. I don't want to go back to Earth, and even if I did, it's doubtful I can make it happen. Nobody is going to help me when I'm the ticket for giving them what they want. My eyes pin C'vest's. "I'm beginning to hate men."

"I've never been so grateful not to have been born female," he agrees, I think. His gaze plays over me in a way I've never seen before. It tightens the hairs on the back of my neck. It makes me wary.

I start to pull away from him. His grip slides from my arms... to my wrists. "Choose."

I try to yank free of him, and can't. He's too strong. My heart begins to beat faster. "No."

"No, what?"

"Just..." I can't *think!*

C'vest's eyes darken to full black. "I've decided for you. Don't fight me and I'll do my best to make this good for you, Stella."

CHAPTER 2

C'VEST

Stella's wild eyes widen further, and her breath gasps from her parted lips. She thrashes to free herself, but I keep her pinned at her wrists, transferring both of hers to one of my hands so I can work the tongue free of my belt.

Being that my belt holds my multi-chambered revolving cylinder pistol, which is six pounds of steel and carbon fiber, it's swift in hitting the floor. The way Stella growls, I know that if she escapes now, it will be a race to stop her from wielding those six pounds and shooting me.

"NO!" Stella begins to shout. Blistering curses follow.

While she vents her displeasure and attempts to escape the upcoming event, I manage to loosen the row of button fastenings that free my organ enough for the purpose it's about to be used for.

I've never partaken in coital relations before. Prior to this marriage-sealing encounter, I've never needed to, and never felt compelled to explore any interest.

As a Yonderin, I'm a species who rears the next generation in underwater laboratories. My kind doesn't breed; we reproduce through samples of genetic material being combined in petri dishes. I don't know any of my kind who copulate like humans. At one time we must have though. And for Stella, I'm going to have to rely on whatever early-ancestral instincts I possess.

So far, my organ is not responding, which I expected. It has never responded, not to any stimuli. Which has always been fine by me. However, circumstances have changed, and I must needs adapt.

I possess electroreceptors, a throwback characteristic for capturing prey in my natural environment. I can detect electrical fields, and find, say, starfish hidden in the sand.

I can also look at a wall and see the energy field of another man on the other side.

I can see into a man's brain, and watch his segments activate. It's a useful tool, for hunting men, for avoiding men. And as far as brain-viewing goes, it's particularly advantageous to watch a skull's activity. There's been more than one deal Baron and I walked away from when a man would make one statement, but the lobe for the opposite function in his brain fired up.

Stella's skull is alight with panic. But I believe I can access the chamber of her brain responsible for excitatory neural activity. By accident and some trial and much error, I've learned I can use a sort of extrasensory force to tap parts of the human cerebrum and beyond. I'm hoping to tap the right spot on hers, to trigger her switch, if you will. I want to engineer the most palatable outcome: I want her to orgasm. Although there is no simple one-step press of a button to make that happen, I am certain I can affect her in positive ways to best accomplish our goals. And although she's not in the right mindset at the moment, they are *our* goals. What I'm proposing is the best solution for her circumstances.

Regrettably, I can't rely on her to see these things with sound reasoning at the moment.

Despite this, I want her to experience the rush of chemicals that will make her body most receptive to invasion, and I want to soften her feelings of intense fear. I don't want to *change* what she's thinking; I simply don't want her to suffer as this is happening.

From my time spent in saloons, I've had the opportunity to study couples' brains during coitus. For females, if they achieve orgasm, activity in their amygdala is subdued. This region of the brain is what helps a human perceive fear. Controlling the levels there would be very useful in this scenario that Stella and I are about to play out. Another area I've observed changes to is the orbitofrontal cortex. This is altered during orgasm, and this affects a woman's impulse control. I'm hoping attention there will help Stella relax, if even marginally.

I begin pulsing around her skull's contents. It's much more difficult than I anticipated.

"YOU STU—*ooo eeerk*," Stella starts off screaming but ends up slurring.

"That is the wrong area of the brain," I murmur to myself and back away from electrically probing that spot.

Stella returns to her cursing of me, and I find I'm relieved. I welcome her to continue, listening for important changes to her speech. When I hit her septal region, she gasps.

I freeze, holding my mental gloved hands aloft.

Across her brain, I watch a burst hit. And then it's like the zone lights up. Purple wires crisscrossing and heating up and creating more and more and more activity.

That's her pleasure center.

I stimulate the neurons with electrical pulses, causing her to sag in my grip at her wrists.

Feeling time ticking at my shoulder blades like an itchy wool coat, I reach for the fastenings on her own trousers.

Weakly, she tries to dodge me, but I keep mentally massaging what I believe I've identified as her nucleus accumbens. I've seen it light up for everything from men partaking in addictive substances to children laughing with genuine happiness. It's an interesting section of the human brain mostly devoted to rewards. I get a mental flash of Stella eating a thickly coated frosted chocolate cake.

Surprised, I stare at the image. Perhaps it's because I'm touching her and I don't touch people—I've never touched anyone while in their mind—but I'm seeing her scene. An actual *scene* inside of her head. It's in her perspective. I'm watching Stella eat a cake she either imagines to be delicious or this is some sort of spectral memory, but that delight and rush she experiences when she partakes in such a confection is actively being triggered. And because it's making her brain thrill with reward chemicals, I keep triggering it.

When I succeed in getting her pants far enough down her thighs that I can access her underwear, she starts to make strange grunting noises. They sound upset, but the comfort food reaction is still playing in the pathways of her mind, and she's struggling to fight against the barrage of those pleasant feelings as I'm forcing her clothing aside.

Finding it difficult to access what I seek, I slip her garment down her legs until she's wearing her clothing around her knees. I locate her clitoris, which is a search more difficult than any diving I've ever done in a brain. My first pass over her organ makes her jump. My second pass I know better what I've encountered, and if she weren't fighting me so hard, I'd get down on my knees to best see the area I need to stimulate. But I'm not going to gamble that she can't manage to kick me in the face even if she is being forced to feel blissfully happy while she does it.

When I succeed in the right combination of strokes to bring her to culmination, the climax causes fireworks inside of her skull contents in nearly three dozen areas. Dopamine and oxytocin will be flooding through her now, and I wonder what effect the happiness and bonding chemicals will have in this situation where I'm forcing our closeness.

Her responses are fascinating to observe, and even with as clinically remote as my own mind is, watching her brain's activity brings about a physical response in my own body. Without physical stimulus of any kind, my sexual organ achieves full rigidity.

I keep mentally tapping the areas in her head that will ensure she's as comfortable and *comforted* as possible, and because I believe the position will allow me the simplest access, I fold her over the arm of the sofa, keep her hands pinned under one of mine, close her hips in, and fit myself to her opening.

Carefully, I press my organ's swollen glans to her arousal-oozing slit. I apply gentle but firm pressure until my glans pops past her tight, slickening walls.

As her hot sheath closes wetly around the head of my shaft, my ability to do anything but take in the sensation of entering her is obliterated. My hips sink against the mounds of her posterior and from outside-in, I'm cushioned and welcomed by softness. I can't electroscan my own brain, but all I can imagine is the inside of my skull splattering with white. For a moment, my eyes don't work; I'm blinded by a pleasure so intense I forget myself.

Stella rears up under me and slams me in the abdomen with her sharp elbow.

"Ooof!" I drop over her and struggle to catch her arm before she can strike me with it again. I grab her other one too, and use them to hold her in place as I very slowly draw my hips back, and...

Dear Creator of the Underwater. I had no idea sex felt like *this*.

Clutching both of her elbows in one of my hands is trickier than her wrists, but I do it and wedge my hand under her body, attempting to locate and arouse her sexual organ's receptors as I begin a slow, rhythmic pattern of motions inside her gripping channel.

I control her brain's responses as best as I'm able. My own responses—and unanticipated desire—shocks me. I stimulate us both, gaining efficiency at arousing her as I stroke myself into her heated grip.

With our mechanical systems being stimulated, chemicals flood us. I direct as much attention as I'm able to the positive workings in her head as my fingers work her externally, and we both achieve an explosive plateau as our critical thresholds are surpassed.

Stella cries out, and I myself make a grunting sort of growl as I ejaculate with enough force to shove her forward. As my hips smack against her rear, her body jiggles in all sorts of places, drawing my eyes as I pin her body with mine, and seed never before implanted in a human floods her receptive channel.

With a final caress over the lit-up areas of her mind, I enjoy a last amazed thrust between her trembling legs.

When I pull back, my cock is shining, wet from her excited juices. Immediately, I want to shove it back inside of her and begin pounding at her welcoming core, but I'm caught staring at the flood of blue fluid that follows my retreat, exiting her tender pink opening. She's glistening and swollen, and our leavings are thick and smell like a unique blend of her and me.

I wasn't sure how I would feel, having Stella for a wife. I wasn't sure if I would like a wife at all. But very suddenly, I'm anticipating more of this, as soon as she'll have me again.

Still facing the sofa's cushions, Stella draws back her foot and kicks me.

CHAPTER 3

C'VEST

We're wed within the hour. During the entire event—not specifically the recognition of our legal binding, but the entire trip (by carriage, so that I could keep her seated beside me, gently nudging areas of her brain, hoping to keep the worst of her unpleasant feelings from overwhelming her) and the meeting of the officiate and signing the proper documents—Stella's expression is... nonexistent. If I could not manipulate areas of her mind, if I couldn't see inside of it to have a guess at what areas are humming with activity, I wouldn't know what she was experiencing. Because outwardly, she's not observable. She's using active suppression so effectively for her outward expressions that she looks... blank. *Everything* outward about her is neutralized.

Taking her hand (and because that is limp, steadying her by the bend at her arm), I assist her up the carriage steps after we exit the office with our paperwork. "Would you like to return home or... shall you move to mine?"

At first, Stella only gives me a dull shrug, as if she's in a numb state. But then I watch a hind area of her brain light up with what looks like a firefight.

"What are you thinking?" I ask, because I can only see the activity. I can't guess at the cause.

Her graceful jaws clench. Her eyes, turning hard, stare straight ahead between our horses' ears. "I was going to say it didn't matter. You've already defiled Baron's... everything." Her gaze cuts to mine. Tries to *cut* mine. "But I don't want to be in your house."

I dip my chin. "Understandable."

"And," Stella continues, gaze sharper than any knife, trying to slice me with her fury, "Baron's ranch hands were looking awfully hungry for his house. Maybe if you move in there, you'll come to some gruesome accident. Let's say the more and more I'm thinking on it, the more I like the idea of going back home."

Ah. So the rear spot of a human's skullbasket is where they hatch their bloodthirsty thoughts. I'll be sure to watch her closely when I see activity here in her mind again.

Walking into Baron's house is no easier than the last time I entered it, with the intentions that I had. And Stella's word-choice of defiled for what I've done—to her, to the union she had already lost with Baron, to their home where his ghost has dogged her day after day since his death—I don't feel at peace with this.

But now Stella is as safe as she can be. She gets to keep her home and she can do anything she did before and anything she feels fit to do from now on. I won't bridle her. She didn't remove Baron's ring from her finger at the ceremony, but she did let me slip on the one I purchased from the officiant. It's this-world's version of the nearly nonreactive, ductile metal her people love: gold. But here, the precious commodity being mined is called *jeren,* and it is ruby red and beautiful.

I wear its larger twin on my own finger. The first and last piece of jewelry I intend to ever put on. I experienced the strangest swell of feelings as I slid it down my left finger until it rested behind my knuckle joint.

Married.

To Baron's Stella.

I never saw this coming. Obviously Stella would never have imagined it either. As she told me earlier, she loved Baron and it was plain to everybody who saw them that this was so. And whats more, Baron cherished his wife. It was easy to see why. She's a handsome woman and a gentle lady and she's capable and supportive and from everything I saw, the ideal partner for a human's other half.

Now she's a Yonderin's other half. Stella is *my* other half.

If I could see into my own brain now, I imagine all of the sectors that would be buzzing with astonishment. That have been buzzing since the morning I knocked on Baron's door, irked with my strange alien friend for not arriving to our meeting with Alvert Galensten. Briefly, I wondered if he was breeding on his wife again, a frequent enough cause of his being late. The mating habits of humans often left me confused. Why do they let themselves touch each other if they know they have other commitments to make? Timed commitments they shouldn't be late for, let alone ones they shouldn't miss altogether.

I knocked on the door of their ranch-style home, with its wide porch, complete with a covered swing that overlooks a section of their river. I expected Baron to open the door with his eyes smiling, his lips pursed in his sheepish expression, and all the areas of his brain turned bright with his heightened activation. His mind would be an Independence Day tradition of fireworks compared to the scans I've made of men during coitus in the saloon. I always attributed the difference to him being a married man, with bonding chemicals traveling strongly in his pathways, against men who only partake in the most casual of encounters.

Now that I've personally coupled with Stella, I don't believe for a moment that my own brain was experiencing a mere casual-lit activity cloud. It had to be its own sort of Stella-storm in my mind.

But instead of finding a ruefully contrite Baron missing his meeting and a suspiciously disheveled Stella, I found a distraught Stella.

And my friend was dead.

His heart gave out, the doctor said. I smelled for poison—I leaned over Baron and sniffed him like a trained hound, although I waited for the doctor to take Stella aside to tell her some-such thing while I examined Baron's body.

I could find nothing amiss. And believe me, I wanted to. I wanted to find an excuse—any excuse—to attack someone. But the doctor's brain showed no hint of deceit when he ruled that the death was due to natural causes. *"He was young, but it happens."* He shook his head. *"One hell of a senseless tragedy though,"* he'd said with genuine regret.

No truer words. Baron was a good man. A fair man. Wise, easy-going, and loyal. He also adopted a slightly inconsiderate alien and taught him how to better operate in the world.

I wasn't ready to navigate the world without him. I never even knew I should worry that the day would come when I'd need to.

I'm certain Stella felt the same.

As we reeled and struggled to believe that Baron was gone, cattle ranch rivals rejoiced. And the opportunity for them to absorb Baron's whole estate lay open before them like a picnic spread.

All they had to do was marry Stella.

And if she didn't agree, then they could take her and have everything they wanted anyway.

As far as Stella is concerned, she probably feels I'm barely an improvement on the vultures circling her husband's assets, but I have every intention of treating her well and giving her all the freedom I'm able. I can also give her happiness artificially whenever I'm close enough to her to manipulate her brain. In time, I hope this is enough to see her genuinely happy.

I round the hitched pair of horses and clamber up into the driver's seat. My prosthetic legs have no sensation but in each limb and cybernetic toe, there are implanted sensors that send biofeedback similarly to a real digit. The technology allows me to sense temperature, walk, step up, jump, run with an accuracy I appreciate, and the tech gets better every solar.

Seeing prosthetics makes some people uncomfortable. Sitting beside Stella, I think of how she never showed—outwardly or in the activity of her mind—that my cybernetic components unnerved her. She's a very accepting lady.

We're both silent on the drive back to her and Baron's home. Our home now.

While I put away the horses, Stella loudly shuts the door of the house. She loudly locks it too, but I had the foresight to grab the house key that was Baron's. I identified it because I could smell him on it, along with pocket lint and horse and Stella. The smell of him was faint, but I caught it as I examined the keys lined up on the hooks by the front door before I escorted her to the office where we signed our marriage documents.

The ranch hands must not have seen me driving the carriage. From the way they creep up to the stall and peer over it, I think they expect to find Stella untacking the horses. The rear sections of their skullbaskets are aglow with a yellow so bright it looks radioactive. Perhaps they think to take Stella unawares as she cares for her mounts. So they're startled to find me, and as I silently flash my ringed finger at each of them (along with my middle finger—an Earthen gesture that Baron taught me some solars ago but I've never quite gotten the hang of; my index finger always tries to rise too), they're stunned. They slink away, their brains whirring as they process that I'm Stella's protection now.

They resume their duties swiftly, with more concentration than I'd wager they've shown in weeks. After all, the temptation for snatching the means to a better station is gone.

At least it is so long as I'm alive.

My life has just become precarious. I make a note to myself to begin setting aside emergency funds in Stella's name starting immediately. Should I die, I'll have an exit package she can escape with, enough to return to her native home planet or anywhere in the galaxy she'd like to flee, if she must. This time, should she become a widow twice, she won't have to cash in cattle or bonds or stocks or sell land in order to have the physical credits to leave. She'll have it in hand.

If I'm dead, I want her safely away from here. We both know she won't be safe alone. Upon being presented viable exit opportunities, I suppose she could take advantage of the option to flee *me* at any time once enough funds are available. I'm strangely reluctant to consider the thought. If Stella leaves, I would... pine for her. Perhaps because she was so dear to Baron, there's something in me that feels connected to her.

Now that we've literally made a connection, I sense our ties everywhere. Bonding emotions are threading through my consciousness. Intimate relationship chemicals are zipping through my system, binding to receptors, altering my feelings.

As I stare through the house's wall at Stella's bioframework, I can see these same changes moving inside her mind too. I also see a welling block in the area of her brain where the signals for intense anger sit.

I'm reluctant to enter the house. But I use my key and am met with a glare so intense I nearly excuse myself and step back outside. I don't because as the man of the manor, my presence deters predators. (Predators other than me.)

I busy myself in Baron's office until dinner, sifting through paperwork and contracts, most of which I already reviewed. Now I'm familiarizing myself with his organization. I'm establishing an idea of what steps I'll take next. It will be a matter of calling associates to the house to show them that I have Stella behind what defenses I can offer. A Yonderin is not popular in these parts, but perhaps providentially, my kind is somewhat feared.

I can give her protection best if I'm alive, but when I sit down across from her at the table for supper, that hindbrain of hers is buzzing with angry yellow-green, especially when she sets my plate of food in front of me. Thus, I commit the unthinkable and decide I'll waste the food rather than risk being poisoned. Just in case she's that level of mad.

When she stabs her steak knife straight down into a T-bone until it strikes into the china plate, I decide she's that mad.

I lick my lips and flick my gaze from her buried knifepoint to her furious face. "If I excuse myself, will it make your meal more pleasant? Or should I stay and provide you with silent company?"

"You can go fuck yourself," I hear her mutter through gritted teeth. But I only hear her because my senses are excellent. The average human would only be keen enough to pick out the decibels of her growling.

I decide to stay still for now. It seems safest. I brush my thumb over the condensation on my glass, hypnotized like usual by the feel of water. I don't miss my ocean home but I do miss swimming. My prosthetics can be submerged, which allows me the ability to swim some. They can also detach, although I no longer have the tail fins I was born with. That loss never fails to make me a little melancholy. But I've gained a lot since I began walking on the terra firma. I don't regret my upgrades.

"Aren't you going to eat?" Stella asks, with acid pooling just under every syllable.

"I've grave concerns that you've poisoned my portions, but I thank you for the offer."

To my surprise, Stella barks a *"Ha!"*

Just one startled shout, not a laugh. The areas for dark amusement are on low-level light in her head though. Which is better than rage, but I can't help but notice there was no denial, thus I'm steadfast in my refusal to consume this meal.

When Stella is done and excuses herself from the table, I thank her for serving me and begin to pick up my plate. She halts me with a, *"Leave it,"* and I murmur thank you before slipping out of the room, exiting the house, and taking up a spot on the porch.

I don't take the swing. I've never sat in the porch swing and have no interest in doing it now. That was Baron and Stella's spot. I take the rocking chair that faces the river, one I've sat in many times.

To my surprise, some time later, I glance over to find Stella somewhat beside me. She's in the swing, also staring out at the river. She's so subdued, I never sensed her approach.

"Are you all right?" I ask.

She keeps staring at the water. "You did something to me. When you were... I felt you in my head. Manipulating my emotions."

I swallow. "Yes. I'm sorry. I was hoping it would help—"

"Can you make me feel that way again?" Her eyes meet mine, the anger at me and her helplessness gone, replaced with a weary, bone-deep emptiness. It's the hollow left behind when a crater obliterates your everything.

Then her regard turns razor sharp. "Not sex. Just cover everything that hurts inside me. Like a blanket to cover a stained sofa."

That she would mention a sofa makes me wonder if she's thinking of the couch I took her on. Maybe we left stains on it, but more likely she thinks of what I did with her as the stain. My senses taste a flattening sadness coming from Stella, and I loosely fist my hands. "All right. I can make you feel some of the same here, now, if you want?"

"Please," she whispers.

I try to recreate the pleasant whirlwind in her mind. This time, she's not fighting me. Eventually, I manipulate her to the point that her lips twitch up in a smile. But it's not natural. It looks reflexive. It looks wrong. Like she's my puppet. I have to turn away and pretend to be staring out over the oxyokes of land as I stimulate a patch of sectors in the midst of her wounded psyche.

Dusk falls. I get up to pace the porch and end up on the lawn. Treading a path back and forth. When I take one step too far, my tether to her breaks and I lose the picture of her mind. She loses my tampering.

Her chest rises and falls, her breaths coming a little faster as she comes back online for herself. It's several minutes of silence between us wherein I wonder if I should ask her if she wants more, but I hold myself back, wondering how much interference is *too* much, when she croaks, "Will you hold me after?"

Throwing her a nonplussed look, I frown. "After what? More of—"

"After we have sex again. Will you..." She looks like she's trying to stomach eating her own tongue. "Please hold me. I think I want to be held."

"Oh." I've come to a complete stop at the foot of the porch stairs.

I consider telling her that I'll hold her irrespective of sexual acts performed, but just the option of sex in the future has me realizing that I may not be able to hold her close without wanting more. I didn't know what I was missing in regards to the act of copulation, and now that I do, I find I want to experience it again. Very much. "Is now a good time?"

Her eyes dart to me.

I spread my hands. "I'm not certain how this works."

Stella blinks hard once, followed by two quick blinks and an open-mouthed exhale. I mount the stairs, coming close enough I can see the areas in her mind for disbelief and resignation.

It's with resignation glowing solidly in her brain when she gets to her feet. "Let's get it over with."

CHAPTER 4

STELLA

I lead the way into the house. Unlike so many nights with Baron, I'm not holding hands with the man who is my husband as we make our way to the bedroom to reconnect. I also don't stall just inside the doorway of the room to seductively undress.

I stop in front of the closet, facing the open doors. My clothes are on the left... Baron's things are hanging neatly on the right.

A lamp comes on behind me. I almost ask C'vest to shut it off, but this is better. I'm not sure I'd want a relative stranger taking me in the dark. I don't think my nerves could handle that.

With numb fingers, I find the hem of my sweater and drag it over my head. I reach behind myself to fumble with the clasp of my bra.

Alien fingers join me, and I freeze.

C'vest doesn't say a thing, and I'm grateful. If he'd asked for permission to undress me, I would have boiled over, the suppressed frustration that he can do anything he wants to me eating me alive. That any man can do anything he wants to me, and I don't have the power to stop him. To change things. It's infuriating. It's stifling. It's unfair.

C'vest's rough-skinned hand smooths down my spine.

The knuckles of his other hand graze over the soft curve of my side. When he reaches my jeans, he pauses. When I don't move, he pinches them at the loops and uses this point to pivot me around until I'm facing him.

I don't tip my head back. I stare at his throat.

His Adam's apple bobs and then he's unfastening the button and zipper of my jeans.

I start kicking them off, hooking my thumbs in the pockets to force them off of myself. There's no passion in my movements. It's undecorated, non-indulgent function. *Get naked. Be passive. Don'tyoudarecry.*

My throat hurts and I feel tears draining or collecting in that spot below and behind the tonsils, whatever happens when your tears fall on the inside and not out of your eyes. When my jeans are kicked free of my feet, I pull my panties off without grace. I step around C'vest and marshal the courage I need to approach the bed.

I loved the man I shared this bed with. And now I'll be under his friend in it. His friend who doesn't love me, his friend who I barely know.

Behind me, I hear C'vest's belt clinking. I hear him set his gun up high, on the shelf in the closet, it sounds like. Probably hoping he can catch me before I sneak out of bed in the middle of the night, bringing a dining room chair to the closet's face so that I can reach to retrieve it and then—

"What are you thinking?" C'vest asks, sounding curious and maybe... wary.

Despite myself, I smile a little. Probably an evil smile. These aren't nice thoughts. "Of what could happen to you once you fall asleep."

"Hm. I surmised as much. There's an area of your brain that radiates with activity when you're having violent thoughts. Specifically ones wherein you consider harming me."

Surprised, I look over at him.

And he's... *naked.*

I've had an idle curiosity as to what's under C'vest's cloths. In that way you do when you see an alien and go, *'What the heck does that one look like?'* Never thought I'd have the opportunity to know. Never craved the possibility.

At his hips, his skin turns to fine scales. His groin is covered with the same scales, as is his considerable... erection.

His penis is long and thick, and it weeps blue fluid. The sides of his shaft are heavily veined. It's interesting. And I guess it's mine.

My eyes force themselves away from the sight of his dick, managing to shift my attention as far away as his cybernetic thigh. His C-legs look like any prosthetic; not *quite* human, but they're sturdy and hi-tech and they get the job done that he needs. Unbidden, my gaze travels over the rest of him (skating over the sight of his penis and heavy sack more than once) until I can make myself meet his face.

He's watching me, taking in my expressions, I think. Or perhaps he's examining my mind.

"Can you tell if I'm nervous?" I ask through stiff lips.

"You are, and yes I can," he confirms.

Inhaling shallowly, I gesture to my head. "Can you make me—" my words die. I'm not even sure what I want to ask for. Is it better to enjoy sex with him or should I silently suffer it? I'm not sure which will make me feel worse.

C'vest's eyes cycle from black to cyborg-blue. "Stella? Do you want me to stimulate you for ease of entry?"

I'm not sure if he means in my head or by my body, but wordlessly, I nod.

Turns out, he means both.

I inhale sharply when he takes me in his arms. He leans back and looks between our bodies, running his thumb down my belly, adding pressure as he crests my mons, gentling his touch when he reaches my cleft and discovers my clit.

In my head, I get hit with an artificial chest full of elation. Not sexual in nature per se. This could be anything. It's pure happiness though, like when you learn you won something you wanted at a raffle. Or when you perform something exceptionally well.

And then C'vest is turning me and pressing me face down on the bed, my hips hanging off the mattress, him coming in behind me.

Doggy isn't my favorite position. Not that it can't feel good, because it has and it can, but because I prefer the intimacy of missionary.

But do I want to be staring into C'vest's face for this?

C'vest comes to a full stop behind me. He draws my hair back away from my ear and leans in to ask, "What's the matter? Up here." He traces a horizontal line above the top of my ear. "You have areas blowing up with color only to have it fade out and explode on opposite sections of your skull's basket. You seem... conflicted about something."

It sounds to me like my brain looks like a Simon Says game, but because C'vest has probably never seen one of those old toys, I don't mention the reference. "Don't worry about it. Just hold me nice afterward, okay?"

There's a significant pause before C'vest gently pets my hair. "I will, Stella."

"Make me feel good again first, please," I ask in a small voice.

C'vest's arm comes around my waist carefully. "Of course."

And just like that, satisfaction floods me, like that first bite of decadent melt-on-your-tongue fudge with savory rock salt on top. As C'vest probes between my legs with his fingers, fumbling with an earnest concentration to please my body, I let the strange pleasure happening in my brain take full root.

When C'vest's thick penis nudges my cunt, I arch my back and enjoy being bombarded with the floating feelings of meretricious happiness. He's hitting me with an effect similar to what I get when I see a basketful of excited puppies.

If I let myself go, it feels nice.

I'm not here, Baron isn't dead, and none of this hurts me.

Physically, it isn't hurting me, and I'm dimly aware of how wet I am as my body welcomes C'vest's luxurious thrust. Instead of being greedy and aggressive—which he could be, he could absolutely take whatever he wants however he wants it and there's no one that cares enough about *me* to stop him—C'vest is treating this encounter like it's *his* delight-on-the-tongue, only he's experiencing his shot of exhilaration in a very different place.

Slap—*suck!* slap—*suck! slap—suuuck!* Our bodies aren't inhibited at all as he begins to pump his hips, my sex reluctant to let him withdraw just as much as it loves the feel of him gliding deep inside me on his return.

In my mind, I'm in a meadow surrounded by a wonder of butterflies. I haven't seen butterflies since I left Earth.

"What *are* those?" C'vest chokes out, panting.

Suddenly, the image disappears, and a man other than my husband is pinning me to the side of the bed, his skin sweaty where he's heavy over my hips, droplets of his perspiration sizzling as they hit my back, his merman-scale-covered ball sack striking me perfectly on that sensitized spot at the top of my cleft as he bangs into me at a pace lively enough to shake the whole bed.

His hips slap against mine with a loud smack (and his balls pop me smartly on my clit again, making my mouth drop open)—

And C'vest leans around me to meet one of my eyes. "Stella?" His finger picks at hairs sticking to the sides of my cheek. When I don't answer, I feel a careful touch in my mind, just as careful as the hand he's using to clear my hair away from my face. And immediately I'm reliving the memory of receiving a high score on a test I studied hard for. The elation I felt. The relief.

Swimming on that same high as if I was back in that classroom, none of the details sharp from that day except for the exultant feelings, the butterfly swarm comes back to me too, just as breathtaking.

"That one," C'vest says, breaking into the image.

It doesn't break the spell though. As if he's petting me inside my head, I keep circling in that meadow, awed beyond reason at seeing all the colors on the fragilest of wings, hundreds of wings.

"Butterflies," I gasp.

"Oh," C'vest murmurs thoughtfully. And very politely, he begins to push inside me again, and a dollop of wetness squeezes out from my stretched lower lips as he forces his way in, the drop rolling down my leg, sticky and hot and rapidly cooling as it escapes our clutch. My wetness with his precum, I assume. And I don't care.

Butterflies and I got an A, and Baron isn't dead, this isn't happening.

His other arm comes under me and bands between my breasts, clamping me flush to his heated and hardworking front, his muscles bunching, contracting as he rides me hard enough to jostle me under him.

Hope blooms in my mind; I'm in the memory of Baron getting down on one knee, having to clear his rough voice twice before he could manage, *"Will you marry me?"*

His voice had cracked, the terror evident in the strong, brave young man who I wanted for my husband in the worst way.

"Yes!" I'd cried, leaping on him.

That exact same elation is as alive in this moment as it was in the real one. I'm so *happy*. I shriek as an orgasm crashes against me like a tidal wave. But at the same time, I'm also aware of myself feeling very, very sad; that same memory that's giving me pleasure is shredding me in the background. Bittersweetness edges in, followed by a cold sort of acceptance.

Baron is gone.

His beautiful proposal may as well have never happened. What we had is over, gone. Destroyed.

My new husband is inside me. Right now. And he just made me come.

He comes too, driven on the heels of my body's pulsing reaction, it seems, clutching me tight enough my ribs creak and the breath whooshes out of me as his weight comes down hard enough to squish me into the duvet.

Cheerfulness overtakes me, and although I don't have a memory to go along with the sensation this time, it's sort of like the mindset I used to get around Christmas when I was growing up. When everything smelled crisp and warm with spices and the outdoors was cold enough to make your skin crackle and everything felt so clean and fresh.

C'vest drags me up on the bed with him, holding me tighter than a panther grips a jungle deer. His mouth goes to my throat like a panther too, his teeth closing against my skin. Rather than bite though, he messily tastes me, licking at my sweat and kissing me. Like he's tired but appreciative and I'm a flavor that heats up his senses.

It's a nice thought, and I like how snugly he's got ahold of me. I feel less like I can break apart this way. But I still hurt. Inside, in a place so deep in my chest no one can reach—not unless his abilities extend to the heart—I ache like crazy.

CHAPTER 5

C'VEST

Stella doesn't speak, and her mood lowers so rapidly I can only watch in dismay as the activity in her mind shuts down like a city block that's lost power.

I struggle to stay awake and I activate all the pleasure centers I have access to while I clutch her in my arms, enjoying the way she feels as I haul more of her against my chest, taking her weight, rolling to my back and bringing her on top of me. My sweat is cooling on her, and where she's not stuck against my areas that have humanlike skin (or a close enough equivalent), she's growing chilly. I rub her upper arm with my palm.

You're lying on the covers, idiot, I realize. I fight to free them, wrenching myself sideways, struggling with the thick blanket as it wraps around my legs, trapping them—a feeling I hate, one that makes panic rise inside of me like some ancient instinct about nets, I suppose. But eventually I free the bedding and rip it back enough to slide us under the covers.

At no time during this process does Stella stir. She doesn't react to me holding her and she doesn't fight my ministrations in her mind. She lets me play her happiness centers with all the permission one gives to a renowned orchestra conductor, if only I had the skill. I can tell that I fumble the sectors and hit on other spots sometimes, but she doesn't complain. Just lets herself feel whatever I can soften her reality with.

I don't let myself fall asleep until she does, and only after she's floating on a blissful cloud, and she's projecting that same image of strange fluttering insects that make her feel delighted.

When I wake up, it's dark in the room, the lamp switched off. There's light emanating from around the partially open door though, and the scent of food and the loud spitting of meat in lava hot lard rouses me enough to get vertical.

I stumble out of the bedroom, and Stella glances up, a spatula in one hand, a strip of bacon sticking out of her mouth, and her eyes go wide.

I follow her gaze, landing below my navel to where I'm not wearing a stitch.

My penis is jutting out proudly as a sailor's marlinspike.

No wonder my pelvis feels tight and hot. Is this what I can expect of married life? Ever since I had Stella the first time, I've been distracted with thoughts of sex with her, and then last night I was consumed with hope that she'd give me a signal that she desired to mate with me too. For someone who didn't understand the appeal of sex or the drive of mating, this is astounding. Staggering, really.

Is this *normal?*

I don't realize that I've voiced the question aloud until Stella makes a noise similar to a choked snicker.

I take my focus off of myself in favor of eyeing her.

Her cheeks go bright, and she turns her attention to whatever is in the odd hinged skillet she's using. She flips the thing closed, glances at the clock over the stove—and then she moves a pan of bacon strips to a cool burner, sets her spatula down and steps to the dining table, bracing her hands on the sturdy split-log planks that form the tabletop.

She glances at me over her shoulder, and her hips lift. "Come on." She spits on her hand and pulls her nightdress up (a garment I've never had reason to notice or have an opinion about until I see how hers hugs her curves) until it sits bunched at the dip over her ample cheeks—and she smears her own saliva between her labia.

Did I think I was staggered before? "Am I dreaming?" My throat is scratchy and my words come out dry.

Stella *laughs.* "Hurry up, or what's in the irons will burn."

I don't even ask if she wants pleasure. Probably with less finesse than if I were solidly conscious, I work her satisfaction centers until she's bursting with high spirits, and for me, I replay how she touched herself to get wet as I shove into her—it was *arousing*—making us both grunt.

She hunkers down over the table and the silverware rattles on the plates, but the construction of the table is good. Solid and heavy as hell so that it barely moves even with the enthusiasm behind my thrusts. I have only a moment to think Stella knew of the table's constitution firsthand—and another moment to shut the thought down that she probably gave herself to Baron this way, just this way, because I wholly believe that he woke up hungry for this affecting creature that was his wife, his vixen of a mate, this morning siren. I give in to the urge to ram into her body, plunging into her like I can breed her right to the other side of the room.

Just as the scent of something burning stings a little unpleasantly in my nose, I explode inside her, making my eyes cross, making our thighs wet when she wriggles until I lift off of her enough for her to free herself in a disconnecting fashion, spilling my fluid out of her as she spins and ducks out from under me and tries to save what's on the stove from causing a housefire.

My body is very confused as she flits around me, filling plates and scraping and pouring things at the stove. I'm a jumble of euphoria and contentment and insensibility. And it's too early for this sort of jumble.

A dry scoff sounds from the stove—it's Stella again, making a sound not unlike amusement. "Sit down," she orders.

Robotically, I do. "What time of the morning is it?"

"It's still night."

"Ah. Are we... is this breakfast or some sort of midnight snack?"

"I guess it's an inbetweenie. I couldn't sleep."

I'm blinking down at my plate when she plops a stack of strange-celled confections onto an already burgeoning pile of strange-celled wedges.

"What's wrong?" she asks, turning away from the stove to peer at me. "They aren't poisoned."

"I appreciate that," I tell her with a nod. "And I'm simply a little flummoxed. About several things. This food is alien, and to add to my disorientation, my eyes are not feeling like they're quite up to speed. It's only slightly alarming me."

"They're black."

I look up at her.

"Your eyes," she says. She grows almost shy, glancing away from me. Fiddling with her hinged cooking tool. "They haven't filled with the blue data lines except for right before we... woke you up."

I give her a lopsided sleepy smile that seems to affect her. If my eyes were working, I might be able to see exactly *what* the effect is. "Thank you for the very welcome wake-up. It was a relief in many ways."

She makes a lighthearted huff of sound and focuses on making more food.

"Are these some sort of baked honeycombs?" I ask.

She frowns over her shoulder and studies me. "They're waffles. You've never seen waffles?"

I shake my head.

"Grab that dish there, that's melted butter. Yep, that one. Pour that on your stack. Now take the berries. Syrup is in the jug to your left, and that's the real maple kind from Earth so enjoy it like it's precious because it is."

"Thank you for sharing," I tell her, touched.

She shrugs both shoulders, pressing her lips together before turning back to the stove. It seems to be a way to express that she's not entirely comfortable.

I decide to try eating in the hopes that I'll wake enough to more accurately read her.

The waffles are delicious. "If these are poisoned," I groan, "it will have been worth it."

Stella laughs. It's short but her tiny burst of happiness is genuine—and with this sound, my abilities have powered up and I'm able to see right inside of her head.

When she sits down across from me, she finishes her first stack without looking at me once.

I don't know what to say to her. I clear my throat and watch her tense—from her brain's activity all the way to her arrested hands on her fork and knife.

"Thank you again for this," I tell her. "Is it all right if we discuss business at the table?"

She relaxes, and her lips part as she inhales. Her eyes never rise to meet mine. "That'd be great. Go ahead."

"Tell me what you want to do, operations-wise. I'd like to focus wherever you'd prefer. Did you want to try a cattle drive before the fall markets close?"

She chews her next bite quicker than her last and forces her mouthful down her throat with a swallow of milk. "Yes," she replies, with a strip of white foam above her lip.

Distracted by it, I reach across the table almost without thinking—and brush it away with my thumb.

Stella goes very still, the glass clutched in her hand, her fork in the other. "Thank you," she says.

I nod, and ruefully I glance down between the edge of the table and my lap. I'm still naked, and now I'm hard again.

"What?" Stella asks.

"I'm certain you don't want to know."

Her eyes bug. "Again? Seriously?"

"I can assure you this organ is very serious."

Stella sets down her milk and her utensil and starts to push away from the table.

"No," I tell her. "Finish your food. I'll have to learn to control this."

"Have you... not had to control it before?" she asks carefully, finally looking at me more naturally—as in, not avoiding looking at me. She's eyeing me like I'm an alien or a cyborg (or both, imagine that, *ha)* as she goes back to cutting up her syrup-covered meal.

"I have not. I've never been interested in copulation before."

Stella chokes on her bite of waffle a little, but recovers. "Ever?"

I shake my head in the negative, watching her mouth, struggling to keep my focus off of her chest. I never noticed the way her breasts swayed before. She's always kept them bound around me before this, but they are free behind her nightdress now and it's distracting.

Stella manages two more bites like it's uncomfortable for her, and then she stands from the table. "That's it. Let's do this and then it's time for you to get out of the house."

"But, you said it's the middle of the night—"

"If you're still awake after this, then you've got more than enough energy to find something productive to do somewhere else." She walks into the bedroom and I think I should tell her that it's fine, but then she puts a knee up on the bed and crawls to the middle of it.

I'm on top of her before she can raise her dress.

I kiss the back of her neck, not caring that her hair is in the way. I'm using my nose to shove strands aside, my hands full of one of her breasts and one of the cheeks of her posterior.

Seeing inside her mind, I'm relieved that she doesn't appear low in mood—she's more surprised than anything. And one of her sections is heating up the harder I nuzzle at her nape.

So I continue to lick her neck until I'm driven to nip it. I stop when she cries out, managing to mutter, "Sorry," before sitting up.

Body slow with seeming reluctance, Stella twists in my grip as much as she's able, one eye meeting mine. "It's fine. It felt... good."

Inside of her head, I see that her pleasure center is shimmering.

"Oh! Well, then..."

I go back to licking and nipping her.

"Suck on the skin," she directs, her breaths shallow and fast.

I do as she says, dazed when her brain's reaction intensifies even more. Delightful; she's absolutely delightful. *"Stella,"* I groan, humping at her affectionately as I move to lave my tongue over her shoulder.

She stiffens a little, and sadness creeps into her brain.

My voice, not Baron's, I realize. Without her needing to ask, I begin to manipulate her brain's centers.

I enter her greedily, gripping her hips and riding her like she's here to teach me bronc busting. But soon the tempo of my body inside of hers slows, because I find myself addicted to rolling my hips in a way that makes Stella moan.

When she first makes the sound, I stop moving, watching her mind's activity for pain.

But it's pleasure she's feeling.

I repeat the motion, again and again, until it's both of us moaning and our vocalizations mingle.

Later, after I hold her until her brainwaves settle, after I rise off of her and cover her with the blanket, I move to my pile of clothes in front of the closet, getting dressed in them even though they scent a little ripely of the day before.

"You can wear Baron's," Stella says, her voice strained. "You're... only a little bigger."

She sounds so sad.

I glance at her, concerned. "No, that's all right. I'll go back to my house today to get my things if you don't mind me moving some here."

"That's fine."

And with that, I retrieve my pistol from high up in the closet. I take hers down too; I stored them together. I turn and cross to the bed, watching her watch me as I approach her. "I'm going to give this to you now."

"Afraid I'll retaliate?"

"A little," I admit.

She doesn't verbally reassure me. But one corner of her mouth quirks—and my heart experiences the oddest, tightest constriction.

"Stella?" I whisper, staring into her eyes as I hand over the pistol I gave to her late husband, my best friend. My best friend who, I'm starting to see for myself, had every reason to care as deeply as he did for this woman. "I think I could fall in love with you."

CHAPTER 6

STELLA

I didn't know what to say to C'vest's statement.

He probably reads the cocktail of stunned guilt that hits me along with that early loop of new-relationship flutters.

And boy does it feel *wrong* that I have any flutters at all. But what's an appropriate length of time for me to accept them? They're bound to happen, despite the sheer speed with which my life has fallen apart and C'vest tore into it.

If this had been allowed to happen naturally, at my own pace...

Well, it probably would have *never* happened.

I don't know when I would have been ready to consider another man after Baron. Maybe never—and I'm not being dramatic. I don't want anyone else, C'vest included. But this is where we're at. And although I could have poisoned him yesterday, C'vest is treating me with such consideration when he takes me that I've truly started to believe that he means me no harm.

Baron used to say that you don't take a man at his word—you take him at his actions.

C'vest seems to be trying to engineer the absolute best situation he can for me, and I'm watching his actions like a mouse watches a hawk.

With his abilities, if he were a cruel man, he could torture me. He could torture me inside and out.

Instead, he's gone to great lengths to... make things easier for me.

I'm starting to think that with C'vest's logical mind, he prepared a pro-con list, decided marriage was the best option for us both, planned out what steps to take if I enthusiastically agreed, and then he planned out steps in case I didn't. At no time did malice enter his thoughts. He's just fixing problems the only way he knows how: a little alien, and completely unrefined. He's a well-meaning bull in a china shop, a slightly clueless one, just like Baron used to shake his head and laugh about.

C'vest leaves the house with a murmured goodbye, and I uncurl from the bed and mince to the bathroom to clean myself up yet again. His out-of-this-world colored cum is extra gloopy and there's an exceptional amount of it. I need to ask him if he knows if an interspecies child is possible. If I'm not pregnant already, we need to put some plans in place unless he wants children.

With Baron, I was always of the mind that if we had them, we'd have them. I secretly knew I'd welcome them, but I wasn't starved to have children, not yet, we had time.

I got my period two weeks after he was gone. For those fourteen days before that, I desperately hoped like I'd never hoped for anything that I was carrying his baby inside of me. Some little piece of him.

Now, with Baron's baby not an option, I'm back to not actively hoping for pregnancy. Yesterday when C'vest first finished in me, I wasn't exactly in a position to refuse him. Let alone order him to use some form of protection. And last night and this morning... well? I didn't care. I just wanted to feel better for one session, and the other two were more like experiencing a surprising street show. Like a tightrope walker or someone juggling fire, or sword swallowing. His stamina is more than a bit of a surprise and if I wanted him like I think he's starting to want me, I'd be thrilled.

It's noon when I hear the front door open. My heart jumpstarts itself as I peek around the living room door, a dust mop in one hand and the neck of a lamp in my other in case it's not C'vest.

It is though. Dressed in a red shirt today, the rest of him in his usual dark colors otherwise, he looks clean and well pressed. But his face is hard and he almost brings the door shut behind him with enough force to make it slam into its frame.

Instantly worried, I ask, "What's wrong?" I look at his empty hands. A pang hits me when I catch sight of his wedding band. *Married. To me. Baron is gone. C'vest is here now.* "Where are your clothes? Did something happen?"

"My things are in the carriage. They'll keep," he says. "And this is what's wrong."

He grabs the front of his trousers, where a massive erection is outlined to vivid perfection.

CHAPTER 7

C'VEST

I seize Stella the moment I enter the house.

Only after having her can I concentrate enough to retrieve my belongings. Moving them in doesn't take long; I don't have many things. And because I was afraid she would become sad or feel threatened to see me move into Baron's spot, I placed my suitcases in the spare room with the intention to unpack later.

I'm wearing one of my nicer shirts, and after I leave her on the bed, I change to a sturdier shirt before exiting. On my way out of the house, I apprise Stella of my plans. "I'm going to take a look at the barn records. If the stock hasn't been vaccinated, I'll start the rounds today. It'll need to be done before they're driven to the sale barn."

"Have a look under this spring's steers too. Make sure they really *are* steers, would you?" Something dark crosses Stella's face.

"You don't think the men have castrated them?"

"I don't think they've even dehorned them."

I stare at her.

She raises her hands, irritation clear in the set of her shoulders. "I put it on the schedule, but I haven't heard or smelled burning happening, which makes me think we might have horns on little bull calves out there. I've gone out to make sure the troughs had water and I can see bovine specks grazing in the distance but I haven't caught the spring calves coming up for a drink, so I don't know what they're walking around with."

Jaw tight, I nod. "Do you want to find out together?"

She empties her dustpan and straightens. Her chin kicks up a notch, and her gaze turns sharp. "You know? That'd be nice. I'd like to get some straight answers."

ONLY HALF OF THIS SPRING'S steers are bona fide steers. The rest are fully intact bulls, and not one of them has been dehorned.

We fire the foreman. It unsettles everybody else, and they listen real well to Stella after that. They also treat Stella with respect while I stand beside her, and she glares them all down fiercely as she firmly takes the reins of her operation.

In deference to the age of the bull calves, she's discussing the use of lidocaine and meloxicam—pain inhibitors—in order to get them dehorned and cut humanely.

Some of the older hands voice disagreement with her on its necessity.

But as Stella points out, the older an animal is, the more stressful the procedures are on their body. And they've waited too long to risk giving them blades and hot irons without being prepared to give the stock aftercare.

She's absolutely correct with her points. Yet some of the men persist in arguing.

"If you're tired of talking, they can start walking," I murmur to her.

Steel in her spine, Stella crosses her arms and smiles at the men. "If you don't want to do it, say the word. You can collect your last check and clean your things out of the bunkhouse."

There are no disagreements with her after that.

But as she stands with her back so straight, essentially toe to toe with the cowboys, she looks fearless and unspeakably appealing, and she carries herself with an authority that lights up lust sectors in several of the ranch hands' brains.

I'm not thrilled. It's hard to fault them when I agree with them, but I'm really not thrilled. I can't decide if they should be punished for involuntary attraction though.

However, as I monitor their brain activity, one ranch hand is not responding to her quite like the others. In his skull, there's also activation in the area for an unsettling aggression. And he's staring straight at her.

I cut my gaze in his direction. "You're done here. You get twenty microts to pack up and then you're gone."

I inhale his scent, tasting it, silently locking it into my receptors. I'll be following him tonight, making sure he doesn't double back here for retribution. Make sure he never gets the chance to mete out that abnormal aggression on any woman.

For one whole heartbeat he looks surprised, then incensed. Inside of his head, guilt flares up. And fear. Not that he knows what I have planned.

And not that he's not alone. Most of the hands shift nervously, studiously not looking at me. As a Yonderin, they're wary enough of me anyway, with rumors 'a mile long' (as the humans I know like to say) on the kinds of supernatural abilities I have.

Some of the rumors have merit.

From all I've overheard though, they don't know the half of what a Yonderin like me is capable of.

The ranch hand I've marked for later keeps his ire to himself, and his eyes show only a little of a predator animal's disquiet as he turns on his heel and marches for his bunk.

"Dawley and Rawlins, you can get out of here too," Stella adds, her jaw tight and her gaze flinty. I part my lips, inhaling their scents too. No sense letting them get together at the saloon for drinks, where they could hatch ideas about the woman who fired them. The woman they must have threatened if Stella is sending them packing. "Fuzzy is the new foreman," she announces. "You got any recommendations on who we can hire to replace these three?"

Fuzzy, a man with a smooth-skinned face (ah, the irony peculiar to cowboys), nods levelly. "Yes, ma'am."

"Good. Let's get to work."

And with that, she opens the calf chute's gate, gets out her box of needles, and I peel the cap off of the first inoculation vial.

CHAPTER 8

C'VEST

We're utterly drained when we get back to the house. We're barely over the threshold when Stella announces, "If you can still get hard, you're going to have to use your hand and imagination. I'm too exhausted to promise you that I can even stay awake enough to watch."

I shake my head. "Curiously, performing scrotal castrations killed all of my desire. I didn't even become hard when you bent over to check hooves."

Stella's amusement center is lit up warmly.

We shuffle into the kitchen. "Hungry?" I ask her.

"Nope," she declines tiredly. "I don't know if I even want to bother showering."

We look at each other and grimace.

"A quick one," she sighs, and trudges for the bathroom.

We both get naked and bathe simultaneously. It isn't a sexual experience in the least, although my eyes do follow her more avidly than I expected I had energy for.

Once dried off, she slides a cotton nightdress over her head. I stay naked. We fall into bed together, groaning.

"I hurt everywhere," she moans.

"I ache in muscles I didn't know I had," I admit.

She has her arm thrown over her face. "We're going to hurt so bad in the morning."

"It's likely."

"Can you reach the lamp?"

Grunting with effort, I sit up and stretch until I can flick off the switch, plunging us into darkness.

To my surprise, my weary eyes watch hesitation play in the threads of Stella's mind. Hesitation and yearning. Then resolve.

And then she rolls onto her side with a pained groan, and slides herself into my arms.

Sleepily, I close them around her, sighing. "This is nice," I tell her.

"Yeah," she agrees quietly. "It is."

I wait for her to fall asleep, and I give in to the urge to silently roar as I rise from the bed—because all of my body is protesting. My vow to dispose of the men as humanely as possible is going to be tested sorely, because not only am I fighting pain, I'm having to leave the warm and soft form of Stella as she sleeps, unaware of my activities to ensure her safety.

Thankfully, she never stirs, not even when I shower a second time, getting rid of the evidence of my hunt. And when I join her again in the bed, she sleepily merges her chest against mine, giving me the curious experience of feeling a human heart in a way completely different from when I gripped the ones in her enemies' chest cavities.

Her organ's gentle rhythm lulls me into the feather-soft realm of sleep.

I DON'T KNOW WHAT TIME it is, but it's still dark when I wake to a sweet-smelling woman with her face tucked into my throat, her arm threaded under my own, her leg thrown over mine—and her tears wetting my neck.

"Stella?" I mumble, concerned. Groggily, I try to scan her brain, but my senses are powered down. "Are your feelings aching?"

A broken sound exits her throat. "Did you kill him?"

All three of them, for you. Because they frightened you. "Did I—" I blink in the darkness, my mind sharpening in increments as I shake off sleep. My eyes begin to work, and my mind catches up enough for me to know that she's not asking about her former employees. I blink again, and I can see the framework of her mind, the signals being transmitted back and forth, her pain turning several areas the same shade of red as the popular Earthen drink known as *sangria.*

I pet her back. "I *didn't,* Stella. I mean it: Baron was my friend. I would never have done that—" *ripping their hearts from their chests and burying them and their belongings under a rubble slide in the bottom of a canyon* "—to him." And I know Baron would have done the same if he'd been alive and knew what was in those men's minds. I find Stella's chin, taking gentle hold of it in the dark, the precision a feat that poses no trouble with eyesight like mine. "I would never have taken him away from you, either." I dare to place a kiss on her forehead, and I exhale in relief when she doesn't flinch away. "I know what you meant to each other. Stella, I'm *sorry* he's gone." For her. And for myself: I never experienced a brotherly bond with anyone—until Baron befriended me.

Despair flares in her, despite the reassertion that I did not kill her husband to take his place. Humans are complicated creatures, especially my new human. I never had to worry about Baron like this. I gather Stella closer and let her weep.

When her tears slow, I place my forehead to hers and rest my palm along the side of her finely boned face. "Do you want me to make you feel better?" I tap her temple softly.

She sighs raggedly. "I feel horrible, but I just... I want to be old-fashioned *comforted.* I want you to make me feel better like this." She reaches down and takes hold of my flaccid organ.

She strokes me to hardness, and for the first time, I enter her while looking into her eyes. In the dark of the room, she can't see me, but I see everything. Every expression that crosses her face—anguish, fortitude, relief.

I move slowly, gripping her tightly, enjoying the feel of her cotton-covered breasts pressing against my chest. Her cotton-covered stomach brushing and rubbing against mine. It's so... intimate.

She shows me the speed and motion she wants from me. When she pushes away to roll to her back, I enjoy the feeling of moving on top of her even more.

Bracing my weight on my forearms, I rock into her with all the wonder I feel. My muscles, strained from the hours-earlier exertion, forget that they hurt. I can't care that they hurt. I just want this. Stella is *beautiful.* Tear tracks and lingering sadness and all. She's strong and beautiful as ever.

And she's *mine.*

"I'm yours," I whisper to her, so low I almost hope she doesn't hear the words. It would kill something inside of me if she's raw enough to reject them.

Instead, she shudders and gulps—and nods. "C'vest..."

I don't make her admit anything she's not ready to. I nuzzle her cheek and brush my face against hers, butting her head gently to the side, and find that my chin fits perfectly in the hollow of her ranch work-toned shoulder. Almost like this silky soft place on her was made to fit a man, just like this.

Everything about her feels good to me. Our skin sticks, and her nightdress is pleasant everywhere it rubs.

She surprises me by jerking it from between our bodies, pulling it up to bare her breasts.

"Touch them," she instructs me.

I raise myself up enough to take a handful, carefully beginning to massage her and learn them. Later, I'll explore and play with these. I'll enjoy them in all the ways she'll let me. For now, I don't want to do anything to disrupt this closeness. I want it. It feels like she needs it.

I think we both do.

"What should I do?" I ask, wondering if she'll tell me to touch more of her body or her brain.

"Grind your pubic bone on my—like *that,*" she moans when I drag myself over her sensitive area.

Rhythmic activity sends her soaring, and I hungrily take in her wide-eyed expression. I murmur to her, "You're magnificent when you're stimulated to culmination."

She's caught in a sexual trancelike state for perhaps thirty breaths, and then she's blinking and sparing me a fleeting grin. "Thank you."

My motions intensify until I reach my own culmination, taking her to an apogee a second time. During the sensory absorption of her climax, her mind isn't flaring with pain.

And she didn't ask me to manipulate her emotions. I was able to give her comfort just like this.

We cling to each other, the flood of excited chemicals in our brain receding, giving each other a startlingly natural sort of solace.

EPILOGUE

STELLA

Three and a half Years Later...

I smile at my toddler, loving his grin as he splashes in the river's gently moving water, his chest supported by my hand.

C'vest is on our baby's other side, hand under his belly, looking at the pair of us with the sort of pride that makes my heart melt a little. More than a little. "There you go, Kaspian. Kick your legs. Kick," he instructs.

I don't need the ability to see inside of C'vest's head to read the joy and delight he's feeling. It's written plainly all over him. As his gaze connects with mine over our son, I feel warm excitement stir inside me, making me think that once Kaspian goes down for his nap, we're going to enjoy a little time for ourselves.

Kaspian Baron Ithor was born with human legs, care of my genes. He inherited fine little scales from his father though, tiny teal ones, that cover him from hips to his adorable little webbed toes. He's cute as a button.

And he's his daddy's little man. Kaspian goes everywhere with his father, even riding in front of C'vest when he's in the saddle.

For C'vest, even though there's no part of Baron in him, Kaspian fills the hole that Baron left when he died.

C'vest does that for me. And Kaspian is the frosting on my cake. The sparkle to my days.

My men make me happy. I love to watch the pair of them together. And I told C'vest that we might need to make another merged copy of ourselves. I'd like a little girl this time, and I told C'vest so.

With a sexy glint in his eye, he'd backed me up to the bed, saying he would do all he could to make me happy.

It's his motto. Two years after we were married, local laws were changed in regards to women's rights in this region of Traxia—largely in part thanks to C'vest's (and my) lobbying efforts. The ruling gained enough popularity to spread to other areas, and women here are finally starting to have a voice and legal protection.

If anything happens to C'vest, I won't ever be put in the position I was. And if we ever have a daughter, she will be safe too.

"Sir? Ma'am?" Fuzzy, our foreman, calls. "We've got a bum calf. Just dried him off."

"This is the only time an orphaned calf is exciting news," C'vest comments.

Fuzzy sweeps his hat from his brow and bangs it against his pant leg, dusting it off, his weathered face smiling in agreement.

"Come here, Kaspian." C'vest lifts him from the water. "We have something to show you."

When Kaspian starts to fuss, sad to leave the river, I feel it's worth ruining the surprise. "It's time for you to meet your baby cow!"

"Cow?" Kaspian repeats with disbelief, flailing on his father's palms in shock.

C'vest raises him onto his shoulders, fitting our son's shiny-scaled legs on either side of his neck. "That's right, Kas. You get your own Nfurian cow."

Kaspian *loves* cows. When I told C'vest to prepare himself for owning a dog—because what child doesn't want a puppy?—our son proved me wrong by endlessly asking us for his very own bovine.

C'vest said as long as it isn't in the house, why not let him raise a steer?

Anticipation thrilling him, Kaspian giggles in excitement, hands on top C'vest's head, enjoying the world from the vantage of his father's broad shoulders as we prepare to meet his newborn pet.

C'vest holds his hand out for mine. I clasp it, stepping into my sandals at the river's edge and touching my shoulder to C'vest's arm as we walk the path to the barn.

"What will our daughter want to raise?" C'vest asks with a naughty tilt of his brow.

Ahead of us, Fuzzy calls out, "Horses," not having a clue that C'vest is mentioning our future daughter as a way to flirt with me.

He also could have no idea how effective the endearingly inexpert attempts to woo me are.

"Probably horses," I agree, smiling and secretly playing out how the next two hours of our afternoon will go: Kaspian will bliss himself out bottle feeding his new calf, and after spending our day off swimming, he's bound to crash hard at naptime—wherein C'vest and I will get some quality alone-time. Maybe enough to make Kaspian a baby sister.

"I'm watching your brain's activity," C'vest warns me under his breath, his hand squeezing mine. "It's arousing my senses."

I squeeze his fingers and smooth my free hand up his arm, leaning into him, biting my lip. "That's good. I'm preparing to take advantage of you when we have a moment to ourselves."

"Only a moment?"

I toss a mischievous look up at him. "Think you'll want more?"

Face serious, eyes earnest, C'vest brings our joined hands up until we're cupping my face. "Stella, I want forever with you. I always will."

My smile for him is soft and tender. "I love you too."

His eyes flare. "I don't think I can wait. Maybe Fuzzy can watch Kaspian."

I grin. "We can't miss out on our son feeding his first ever pet."

C'vest's eyes turn circuitry-blue and his gaze turns inward. "I've never tried it, but perhaps I can locate a sleep-switch in our offspring's brain."

"Don't you dare."

C'vest's hand curls tighter around mine and he cuts me a glance. "I wouldn't. But I am wishing I wasn't so against the idea of creating a child alcoholic. Half a dram of whiskey and—"

I disengage our hands and whack him on the arm.

Watching it happen from his perch, Kaspian squawks down in surprise before giggling, and Fuzzy glances back at us and shakes his head. He calls, "If you two are going to keep getting sweet on each other, I can keep an eye on Kas. Y'all could slip into the barn office to do some 'paperwork.'"

"And that," C'vest declares, "is why you're getting a raise." He slings his arm over my shoulders and tugs me against his side.

I slide my hand under his shirt intending to lightly pinch him, but he shies away from me like a nervous stallion, making Kaspian cackle and clap with glee.

C'vest shoots me a sideways glance and taps low on his skull. "I saw this spot light up on you again. You always get dangerous when you have activity here."

"Since you've escaped me, what's lit up in my head now?"

"Amusement." His eyes heat. *"Arousal,"* he adds, mouthing the word.

I let him catch me at the doorway of the barn. And when Kaspian's calf has taken in half of a bottle and Fuzzy gives us a knowing nod and a good-natured smirk, I let C'vest drag me into the office where the thin walls require the use of his hand clamped over my mouth.

As my body shudders in pleasure under his, he whispers in my ear, "I love you, Stella."

THE END

NOTE FROM AMANDA

Did you like this story? I'll be on the lookout for reviews to see what you thought—and if you take the time to leave one, I appreciate it! *Thank you so much* for reading! =D

Love and Otter Hugs <3

AND A RIB-SQUEEZING HUG FROM A RAKHII!!!

~Amanda ♥

Newsletter: http://eepurl.com/cR_CNf

https://www.bookbub.com/authors/amanda-milo

https://amandamilo.com/

https://www.facebook.com/AmandaMiloAuthor/

About the Author

Amanda Milo is a collector of the randomest trivia. *Did you know that Kiwi fruit plants have separate genders? You need both in order to make Kiwi fruits happen. Isn't that cool??*

She's concerned about river otter bite pressure—she hasn't had a chance to test this out, but frankly, this is the part that's holding her back from appropriating and testing the relocation (aka wildlife theft) of a small family of adorable river otters.

…To the bathtub. (They're basically like slick-furred rubber duckies, but with lots of teeth, right? Right.)

Extended contemplation of this plan has led to the permission to adopt more ferrets, which makes her very happy. So does her extensive, wacky-patterned, thigh-high sock collection—though ferrets, it must be noted, do not play well with pretty socks. The crazy, clawed thieves!

She invites you to hang out with her in the *Amanda Milo's Minions* Facebook group. (She didn't name the group! XD Readers have great senses of humor!)

Thank you for picking up this book. Amanda hopes that you had a lovely time. ♥

www.ingramcontent.com/pod-product-compliance
Lightning Source LLC
Chambersburg PA
CBHW021138130726
47988CB00003B/1362